For Jennifer, Julia and Moritz

Copyright © 1997 by Nord-Süd Verlag AG, Gossau Zürich, Switzerland.
First published in Switzerland under the title Der Sternenbaum.
English translation copyright © 1997 by North-South Books Inc.

First published in the United States, Great Britain, Canada,
Australia, and New Zealand in 1997 by North-South Books,
an imprint of Nord-Süd Verlag AG, Gossau Zürich, Switzerland.

Library of Congress Cataloging-in-Publication Data is available.
A CIP catalogue record for this book is available from The British Library.
ISBN 1-55858-741-1 (trade binding) 10 9 8 7 6 5 4 3 2 1
ISBN 1-55858-742-x (library binding) 10 9 8 7 6 5 4 3 2 1
Printed in Belgium

For more information about our books, and the authors and artists
who create them, visit our web site: http://www.northsouth.com

The Star Tree

Written and Illustrated by Gisela Cölle

Translated by Rosemary Lanning

North-South Books

NEW YORK · LONDON

IN A LITTLE HOUSE, in a big city, there once lived a very old man. He had lived in this house for as long as he could remember. He had watched the city grow bigger and bigger, seen it swallow up parks and gardens, seen skyscrapers rear up and supermarkets sprawl.

The people who lived in the skyscrapers knew nothing of the old man. Most of them didn't even know each other. Every morning they hurried off to work, and at night they came home exhausted. They let whole days go by without once looking up at the sky.

One winter night, a few days before Christmas, the old man sat in his little house, thinking sadly of Christmases long ago.

In those days, friends and family gathered around the stove to tell stories and sing carols. The children would make gold stars and hang them in the windows to welcome visitors.

The old man thought that he still had a roll of gold paper somewhere in the house. He searched in cupboards and drawers until at last he found it. He picked up a pair of scissors and cut out a star, then another and another.

Then he stood up and went to the window.

The old man looked out at the gaudy Christmas
decorations slung across the streets, and he sighed.
Would anyone notice his paper stars, he wondered,
among all the garish, glittering lights? He decided
to take the stars out into the countryside, where
it was darker and his stars would show up better,
reflecting the gentle light of the moon.

Outside, the wind was rising. It whipped up the ends of the old man's scarf, and scattered some of his stars.

In the city, the wind rattled and ripped the gaudy Christmas decorations. Then it tore down the power lines.

All the lights went out, and
the loudspeakers stopped blaring
their jangly Christmas songs.

The city lay silent and dark.

The old man walked through the silent streets, past the tall buildings, past the darkened windows and the locked doors.

Darkness and silence were new and strange to the people of the city. They huddled indoors, afraid to go out.

The old man walked on and on, out of the city, across the fields, and up the highest hill.

As he reached the top, the storm began to lose power. Then at last the wind drove the clouds away, and a huge December moon appeared in the sky.

"Look, there's a man in the moon!" cried the children.

"No, no," said their parents. "The man in the moon doesn't exist, except in nursery rhymes!"
Then they saw a figure outlined against the moon, with a trail of gold at his feet.

They were so glad to see a light that they
took their children by the hand and led them
out of the city. They walked over the silent,
snow-covered fields and up the hill.

When they reached the top, they saw the old man hanging gold stars on a tree. The stars twinkled in the moonlight, and cast a golden glow on the bare branches and the snow beneath.

Everyone stopped and stared in wonderment.

Then one of the children began to sing a Christmas carol, quietly at first, then louder as the others joined in. The old man turned around when he heard the singing.

"This feels more like Christmas!"
he said, and he began to sing too.

Then the old man took the rest of the stars from his basket and gave one to each of the children. He was happy to share once more the simple pleasures of Christmases long ago.

The children carried the stars back into the city and hung them in their windows. Other children saw the stars and made some of their own.

Soon the whole city
shone with the glow
of Christmas stars.